In a stressful family situation, children can find it difficult to express their feelings. This book provides a wonderful opportunity for children and parents to talk about their feelings together. It is beautifully scripted, with poetic language, and illustrated with evocative pictures that could lead the way to open dialogue about fighting in families. It confirms for children many of the feelings they experience during parental fights—the fear, isolation and sadness—and yet ends with an uplifting resolution. Not only families but also mental health professionals can use this impressive book as a jumping-off point for healing discussion.

—Dr. Barbara Kezur,
Ph.D, Psychology
Humanistic Psychology Institute, California

For Donna, Emily, Suzy,
Christopher, and Charlotte KW

For the National Federation
of Badger Groups CW

This Americanized Edition of *When They Fight*, originally published in English in 2000,
with the title *Good Day, Bad Day*, is published by arrangement with Oxford University Press.

If you would like to help badgers in Britain, please write to
The National Federation of Badger Groups,
15 Cloisters Business Park, 8 Battersea Park Road,
London SW8 4BG, England.

White, Kathryn (Kathryn Ivy)
When they fight / Kathryn White ; illustrated by Cliff Wright.
First Edition.
p. cm.
Summary: A young badger describes how bad he feels when his parents argue
and how good he feels when they are friends again.
ISBN 1-890817-46-5
[1. Badgers Fiction. 2. Fighting (Psychology) Fiction. 3. Parent and child Fiction.]
I. Wright, Cliff, 1963- ill. II. Title.
PZ7.W58376Wh 2000
[E] — dc21
99-37957 CIP

Library of Congress catalog card number: 99-37957
Jacket design: Billy Kelly
Printed in Hong Kong

For games, links and more, visit our interactive Web site:

www.winslowpress.com

When They Fight

Kathryn White
Illustrated by Cliff Wright

Winslow Press
Delray Beach, Florida • New York

When they fight,

the world shakes.

The house quakes.

Beasts roar

and beat on the door.

It gets dark, and I am lost.

It gets cold,
and I shiver.

Mighty monsters
make me quiver.

I am a ship in
stormy seas.

I am a kite, blown
away in a breeze.

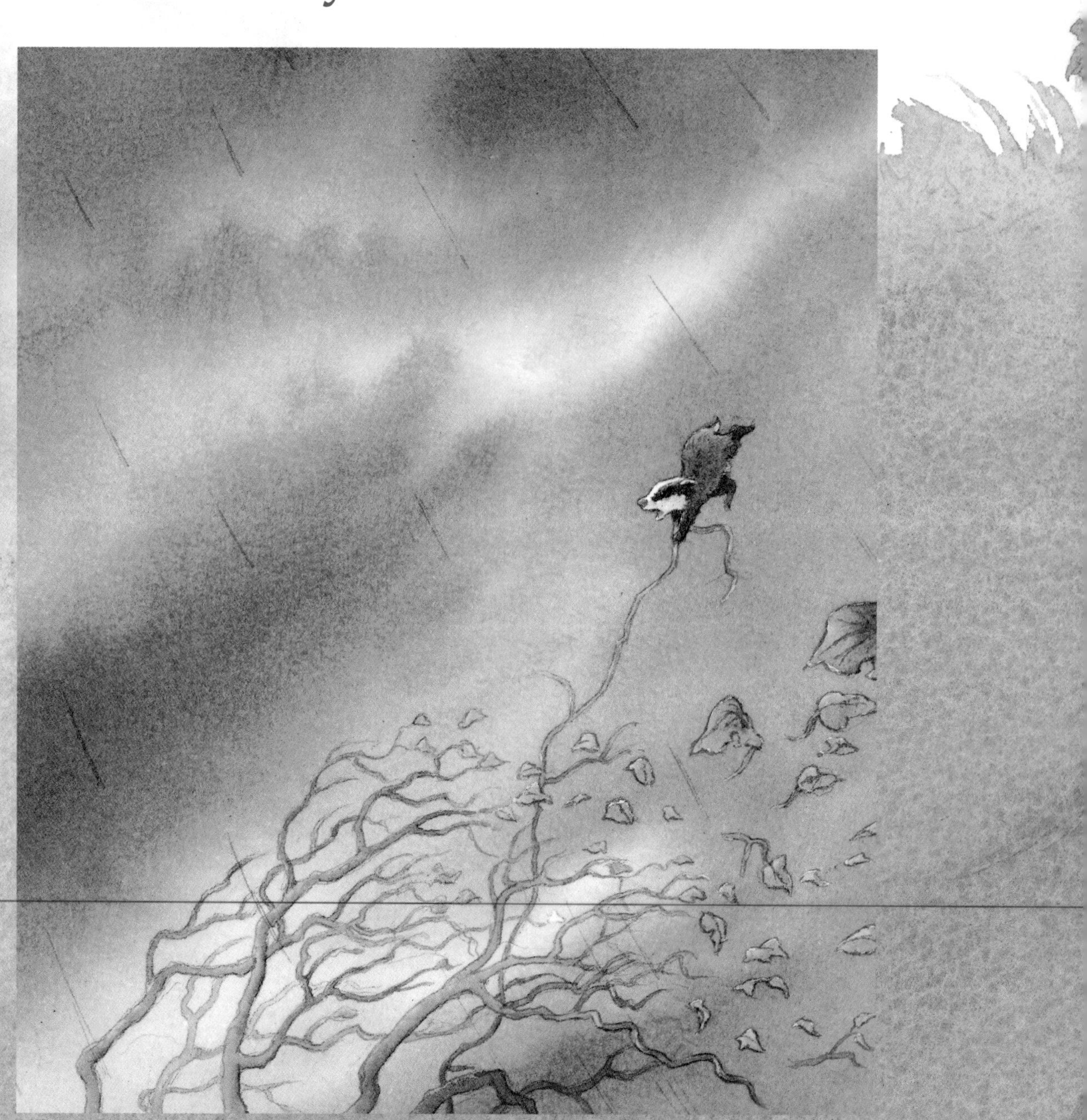

Will I ever see
home again?

I feel lonely.
I feel sad.

When they are friends,
the sun comes out.

I float on the clouds.

I am as strong as a lion.

I can sing. I can dance.

I can shout. I can do anything.

I can jump as high as the moon.

I can run as fast as a tiger.

The world smiles.

I am safe.
I am warm in a cozy nest.